Tamara
the Tooth
Fairy

by Daisy Meadows

ORCHARD

www.rainbowmagic.co.uk

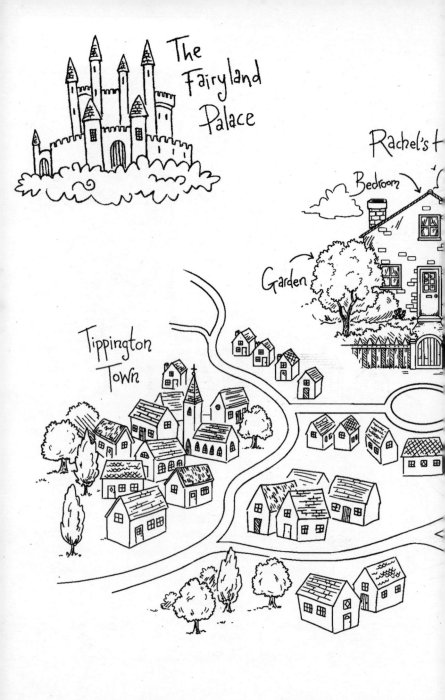

The Fairyland Palace

Rachel's

Bedroom

Garden

Tippington Town

Tamara
the Tooth
Fairy

To Aleka Sumatpimolchai with lots of love

Special thanks to
Rachel Elliot

ORCHARD BOOKS
338 Euston Road, London NW1 3BH
Orchard Books Australia
Level 17/207 Kent Street, Sydney, NSW 2000
A Paperback Original

First published in 2012 by Orchard Books

HiT entertainment

A CIP catalogue record for this book is available
from the British Library.

ISBN 978 1 40831 687 0

1 3 5 7 9 10 8 6 4 2

Printed in Great Britain

The paper and board used in this paperback are natural recyclable
products made from wood grown in sustainable forests. The
manufacturing processes conform to the environmental regulations
of the country of origin.

Orchard Books is a division of Hachette Children's Books,
an Hachette UK company

www.hachette.co.uk

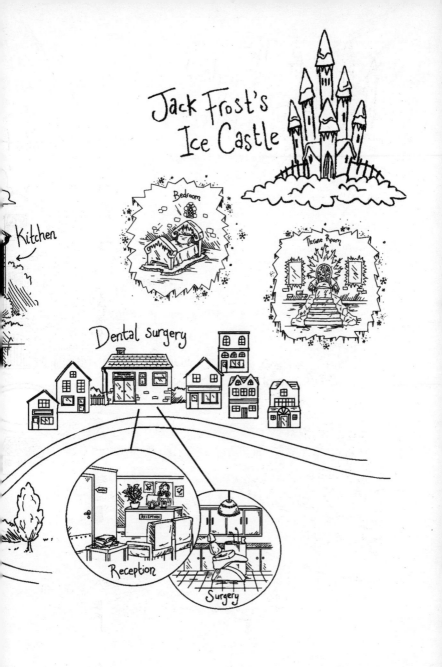

Jack Frost's Ice Castle

Kitchen

Bedroom

Throne Room

Dental surgery

Reception

Surgery

Jack Frost's Spell

My tooth is aching once again.
But Ice Lords shouldn't suffer pain!
I've thought it through, and now I'm sure
Tamara has the only cure.

She makes our wobbly teeth a game,
So I've decided she's to blame.
Bring all her magic things to me,
And stop this toothy agony!

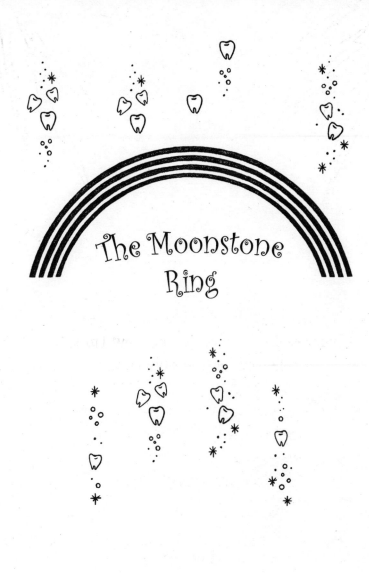

The Moonstone Ring

Contents

Tooth Trouble

Rachel Walker opened her bedroom window and leaned out, gazing up at the starry sky. She took a deep breath of fresh air, and smiled happily.

"This is going to be the best summer ever," she said aloud.

Her best friend Kirsty Tate had arrived that morning to stay with her in Tippington. Three long, sunny weeks stretched ahead of them. Rachel couldn't wait to find out what adventures were waiting to be enjoyed. Whenever they were together, the most exciting and magical things seemed to happen.

She heard her bedroom door open and turned around. Kirsty came in, holding something small in the palm of her hand.

"Rachel, guess what?" she said. "My wobbly tooth has finally fallen out!"

"That's brilliant!"

12

said Rachel. "We can put it under your
pillow tonight, and let the Tooth Fairy do
her work."

She drew the curtains and both girls
changed into their pyjamas. Then Kirsty
put her tooth under her pillow, and
patted it down happily.

"We've never met the Tooth Fairy, have
we?" she said, climbing under the covers
and snuggling down. "I wonder what
she's like."

Rachel and Kirsty had a very special secret. They knew many fairies, and had visited Fairyland many times. Sometimes the Ice Lord, Jack Frost, made terrible mischief with his goblins. The girls had often helped the fairies foil his plans.

"Perhaps we'll wake up when she comes to swap your tooth for a coin," said Rachel. She got into bed and yawned.

"The Tooth Fairy is so quiet that she never wakes children up," said Kirsty.

Rachel smiled and turned out her bedside light. It had been a long day, and within a few minutes both girls were fast asleep.

When Rachel's alarm went off in the morning, she sat up and looked eagerly across at the bed where her best friend was sleeping.

"Kirsty, wake up!" she said. "See what the Tooth Fairy has brought you!"

Kirsty sat up too, and lifted her pillow. Then her shoulders slumped.

"My tooth is still here," she said in a disappointed voice.

Rachel jumped out of bed and came over to sit on Kirsty's bed. Sure enough, the little white tooth was still lying on the sheet.

"The Tooth Fairy is probably confused because you're staying here instead of at home," she said, putting her arm around Kirsty. "I expect she'll come tonight."

"Perhaps she left the coin and forgot to take the tooth," said Kirsty, picking up the pillow and shaking it. "Or maybe the coin got stuck inside somehow?"

As she shook the pillow, the girls heard a faint tinkling sound. Then, with a sparkling whoosh, a tiny fairy came shooting out of the pillowcase. She did three somersaults through the air and landed on Kirsty's bedside table. She was wearing a pretty ruffled skirt with funky red boots and a spotty top, and her long golden hair coiled over her shoulder.

"Hello, Kirsty and Rachel," she said.

"I'm Tamara the Tooth Fairy."

"Hello, Tamara," said Rachel. "Are you here to take Kirsty's tooth?"

"I wish I could say yes," said Tamara, looking upset. "But Jack Frost has been causing trouble again. Girls, I've come to ask for your help."

"What's happened?" asked Kirsty.

"I'll show you," said Tamara. "Queen Titania has used her royal magic to find out what happened."

She waved her wand towards the

18

mirror hanging on the wall, and the surface rippled. When it was smooth again, it no longer reflected Rachel's bedroom. Instead, the girls saw Jack Frost's face scowling at them!

Scaredy-Jack

Jack Frost was sitting on his throne, with a hand clamped to the side of his face. He was moaning and groaning at the top of his voice. Goblins scurried around his feet, cringing as he bellowed.

"None of your stupid cures work!" he roared. "I've rubbed bits of garlic and potato and ice cubes and pepper powder into my gums, and it's all a load of rubbish! My tooth still hurts!"

He kicked out
at a tray that a
warty-nosed
goblin was
holding, and
a toothbrush,
floss and
toothpaste
flew through
the air. The
goblin got down on
his hands and knees to pick
them up.

"Perhaps you should go to see the
dentist," muttered the goblin.

At once, the whole throne room went
silent. Jack Frost sat up very straight. The
other goblins backed away.

"*What* did you say?" hissed Jack Frost.

The warty-nosed goblin looked around and realised that he was on his own. His bottom lip started to tremble.

"N-nothing," he babbled, scooping everything onto his tray and crawling out of reach of Jack Frost's bony feet.

"I never want to hear the word 'dentist' in this room again!" screeched the Ice Lord.

"But how are you going to get rid of your toothache without a den…er… without help?" asked the goblin.

"It's that Tooth Fairy!" Jack Frost snarled, banging his fist down on the arm of his throne. "If I had her magic, I bet my teeth would be perfect!"

Suddenly a cunning light crept into his eyes.

"You, goblins, come closer," he said. "I've just had a brilliant idea. Only the Tooth Fairy's magical objects will stop my tooth from hurting, so you know what that means, don't you?"

24

The goblins scratched their heads, looked at one another and shrugged.

"You're going to steal them for me!" shouted Jack Frost.

The image on the mirror rippled again, and then disappeared. Tamara turned back to the girls with a heavy sigh.

"And that's exactly what happened," she said. "I sleep in the day and work at night. In the middle of the day yesterday, the goblins sneaked into my home while I was asleep, and took all three of my magical objects."

"That's awful," said Rachel. "You poor thing!"

"Without them, I can't do my job," Tamara went on.

"What are they?" asked Kirsty.

Tamara used her wand to draw pictures in the air, just like a sparkler on Bonfire Night. The first picture showed a delicate, shining ring.

"The moonstone ring glows when it is close to loose teeth," she explained. "It guides me towards the children who are waiting for me."

The second picture showed a small coin with a star engraved on it.

"The endless coin allows me to place money under every pillow – I can't take teeth without it," said Tamara. "I put it under the pillow and wave my wand. Then the coin is magicked back to my pocket along with the tooth, and ordinary money appears for the child to find when they wake up."

The third picture was a velvety drawstring pouch.

"The enchanted pouch contains all the teeth I've ever taken, ground up into magic fairy dust," said Tamara. "It is very rare and powerful fairy magic."

"Is there anything we can do?" Kirsty asked.

"I hope so," said Tamara. "I came to ask you for help. Without the moonstone ring, I can't even find the children who need me."

"So that's why you didn't collect Kirsty's tooth," said Rachel.

Tamara nodded sadly. Just then, the girls heard Mrs Walker calling them.

"Girls, time for breakfast!"

As quick as a flash, Tamara zoomed under a lock of Rachel's hair, and the girls went downstairs. Mrs

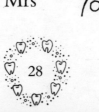

Walker was carrying a pile of magazines through to the hall.

"I've been having a good clear-out of all my old magazines," she said. "I was wondering if you would take them down to the recycling bins in town for me?"

"Of course we will, Mum," said Rachel at once.

The girls went into the kitchen and sat down at the breakfast table.

"After we've recycled the magazines, we can start searching for the moonstone ring," said Kirsty in a low voice. "We have to stop Jack Frost spoiling things for children all over the world!"

The Ring Leads the Way

After breakfast, Rachel and Kirsty got dressed and put the magazines into two large bags. Then they set off to walk into town. It was early and there weren't many people around. They could only see three small boys ahead of them, wearing baseball caps. One of them had a football under his arm.

Tamara was hiding inside Kirsty's shirt pocket, but she popped her head out as they walked past the library.

"Girls, I can sense that my ring is very close," she said. "I feel tingly all over!"

"I wonder where those boys are planning to play football," said Rachel thoughtfully. "They're going in the opposite direction from the park."

At that moment, the sun came out from behind a cloud, and it shone down on the three boys. Something sparkled on the tallest boy's finger, and Tamara gave a yell of excitement.

"That's the moonstone ring!" she said. "I'd know it anywhere."

"That means those boys are goblins," said Kirsty with a frown. "Let's follow them."

The goblins walked towards the centre of town. They seemed to be arguing.

The ring flashed brightly in the sunshine as the tallest goblin waved his hands around. The girls kept as close as they dared, hoping that the goblins wouldn't look around.

At last the goblins turned down a side street.

"Where can they be going?" wondered Rachel.

They peered around the corner and saw that the goblins had stopped. They were standing outside Tippington Dental Surgery, and the girls could hear what they were saying.

· TIPPINGTON ·
DENTAL · SURGERY

"The ring's definitely telling us to go in here," said the tallest goblin. "It's gleaming so brightly I can hardly look at it."

"What if it's leading us to those pesky fairies?" said the second goblin, who was wearing sunglasses that were far too big for him.

"It's leading us to lots of teeth, stupid," said the third goblin in a very squeaky voice. "That's what Jack Frost said it does. He needs as many teeth as possible."

"What for?" asked the second goblin.

"Wake up!" screeched the tallest goblin. "Jack Frost is going to grind them up to make magic dust, and that will stop his toothache. He says that the stupid pouch doesn't work, so he needs more teeth to grind up."

"Of course it doesn't work," said Tamara in a low voice. "It's not *meant* to cure toothache. It's a charm that helps dentists do their jobs!"

"Get out of my way," said the second goblin at that moment.

He elbowed the other two aside and ran up the steps into the surgery. The other two goblins followed, still arguing loudly.

"Oh no, they're bound to cause trouble in there," said Kirsty.

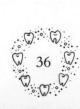

"We have to stop them."

"I must get my ring back," said Tamara
in an urgent voice, hopping from one
foot to the other inside Kirsty's pocket.
"We're so close – we can't let them get
away!"

"We're *not* going to let them get away,"
said Rachel. "We've got
the perfect reason to
go into the surgery."

She held up one
of the bags of
magazines that she
was carrying.

"Of course!"
Kirsty exclaimed.
"Dental surgeries are
always wanting magazines for people to
read while they wait."

"We can go in and donate the magazines – and have a good look around at the same time," said Rachel.

"Brilliant plan!" Tamara cried, and her wand gave an excited golden fizz of fairy dust.

"Keep out of sight," Kirsty reminded her. "The receptionist mustn't see you."

Tamara ducked down again, and Rachel and Kirsty hurried up the steps and through the frosted glass doors. A stern-looking receptionist glared at them down the length of her nose.

"Do you have an appointment?" she demanded. "The dentist doesn't come in until ten, you know."

"No, we don't have an appointment," said Rachel politely. "But we have two bags of magazines. Would you like them for the waiting area?"

The haughty receptionist gave a flicker of a smile.

"That's very kind," she said.

"I'll go and put them on the tables for you," said Kirsty quickly.

She took Rachel's bags and winked at her.

"Keep her talking," she whispered. "I'm going to find those goblins!"

The Great Goblin Tooth Hunt

RECEPTION

Rachel stood beside the reception desk and blocked the receptionist's view of the waiting area. Kirsty put the magazines on the table and then looked around. The door to the surgery was slightly open. She stepped closer, and heard a muffled giggle coming from inside.

"That was a goblin!" she heard Tamara whisper. "Let's investigate."

"OK," Kirsty replied in a low voice. "The dentist doesn't come in until ten. That gives us half an hour."

Kirsty glanced over at her best friend. Rachel was chatting to the receptionist about the Tippington summer carnival.

Kirsty pushed open the surgery door and peeped inside.

CRASH! BANG! CLATTER! The goblins had turned the surgery into a disaster area. Cupboards were open and dental equipment was scattered on the floor. The tallest goblin was sitting in the chair, playing with the mouth wash tap, and the goblin with the squeaky voice was giggling as he hung upside down.

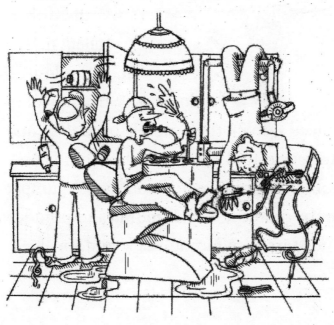

"Those naughty goblins!" Kirsty exclaimed.

Tamara looked out of the shirt pocket and gasped. The tallest goblin, now wearing sunglasses, had a mouthful of pink rinse and was spitting it at the others. As the girls watched, he sprayed the last drops over the squeaky-voiced goblin, then picked up a drill and started to make holes in the wall. The goblin dripping with mouthwash jumped up to grab the low-hanging lampshade, and started swinging back and forth.

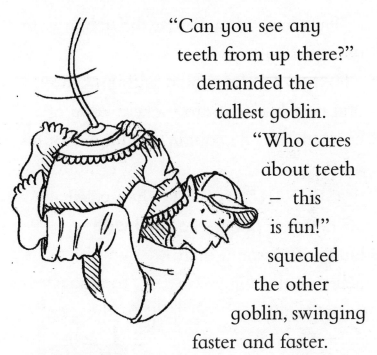

"Can you see any teeth from up there?" demanded the tallest goblin.

"Who cares about teeth – this is fun!" squealed the other goblin, swinging faster and faster.

"You'll care about teeth when Jack Frost catches you!" said the tallest goblin, shining the dentist's light into the eyes of the other one.

"OW!" screeched the goblin. "Stop it!" He let go of the lampshade and crashed to the floor.

"Hey, look at me!" said the goblin with the squeaky voice.

He had filled a mould with pink wax, and now bit into it to make a copy of his teeth. But he couldn't pull it out of his mouth!

"GEHRIRROWWW!" he wailed.

The other goblins cackled with laughter, clasping their bellies and rolling around on the floor. The tallest goblin rolled into a tall cabinet, which burst open. A cascade of loose teeth rained down on him.

"Got them!" he squawked.

The goblins fell on the teeth, scooping up as many as they could carry.

"We have to stop them!" cried Tamara.

She zoomed out of Kirsty's pocket and into the surgery.

Kirsty followed her and stood with her back against the door.

"Stop!" she demanded. "Those teeth don't belong to you. Put them back!"

"No way!" snapped the tallest goblin.

"These teeth are for Jack Frost, not for silly humans and pesky fairies."

Kirsty thought quickly. She had to think of a way to get Tamara's ring back, and to stop the goblins from stealing the teeth. She winked at Tamara to show her that she had a plan.

"Jack Frost won't want boring old teeth like that," she said. "Tamara could use her magic to make you some teeth that are really fun. Don't you think Jack Frost would like special wind-up teeth that jump around and chatter on their own?"

"That sounds brilliant!" gasped the goblin with sunglasses.

"Forget about those teeth you're carrying," said Kirsty. "All you have to do is give us that ring on your finger, and Tamara will magic you up three wonderful new sets of teeth."

"Of course I will," said Tamara. "Well, goblins? Will you agree?"

Gifts for the Goblins

The goblins looked at one another.

"I bet Jack Frost would be really pleased with us if we brought him three whole sets of teeth," said the one with the squeaky voice.

"Yes, and he won't need the ring when he's got lots of teeth," the tallest goblin thoughtfully agreed.

They all turned to Kirsty and Tamara, and nodded.

"It's a deal!" they said together.

They all dropped the dentist's teeth on the floor. Then the tallest goblin took off the ring and held it out. Tamara fluttered over to him and took it. Instantly, the ring shrank to fairy size, and Tamara slipped it onto her finger.

"Give us our teeth!" demanded the goblin with sunglasses.

Tamara smiled, and then waved her wand and said a spell.

"*Chatter, natter, grind and chew,*
These goblins all want something new.
Give each one a set of teeth
To take back to
their icy chief."

There was
a golden,
sparkling
flash, and
then each
goblin
found a set
of plastic
wind-up teeth
in his hand.

They giggled and
squawked with
delight as the
teeth jumped
around and
chattered.

"Let's
get out of
here before
those tricksy
humans try to
stop us!" shouted the
goblin with the sunglasses.

One by one, the goblins leaped out of
the open window and scampered off.
Tamara tidied up the surgery with one
swish of her wand, and then she darted
into Kirsty's pocket and Kirsty walked
back out into the waiting area.

"All done," she called to Rachel, giving her the thumbs-up.

"Off you go, then," said the receptionist. "Thank you for the magazines."

Rachel and Kirsty hurried down the steps and hugged each other. Tamara popped out of Kirsty's pocket and wiggled her hand around in delight. The moonstone ring flashed in the sunshine.

"You got the ring back!" Rachel exclaimed. "Well done!"

"Does this mean you can take my tooth now?" Kirsty asked.

"I'm sorry, Kirsty, but I can't," said Tamara. "It's magically impossible for me to take a tooth without replacing it with the endless coin – and the goblins still have that."

"Then we'll just have to find the endless coin as fast as we can," said Rachel, giving her friend's hand a comforting squeeze.

"Put the tooth back under your pillow," Tamara told Kirsty. "You have both been so wonderful. I'm sure that if you help me, I'll soon find the endless coin and the enchanted pouch."

"Of course we'll help you!" said Kirsty.

"I have to go back to Fairyland now," said Tamara, "but I'll be back as soon as I have any news."

As the moonstone ring gave a final flash, she twirled into the air, faster and faster, and then disappeared in a puff of golden fairy dust.

Rachel and Kirsty looked at each other and smiled.

"Let's go home and put that tooth back under your pillow," said Rachel. "I've got a feeling that Tamara will be able to take it very, very soon!"

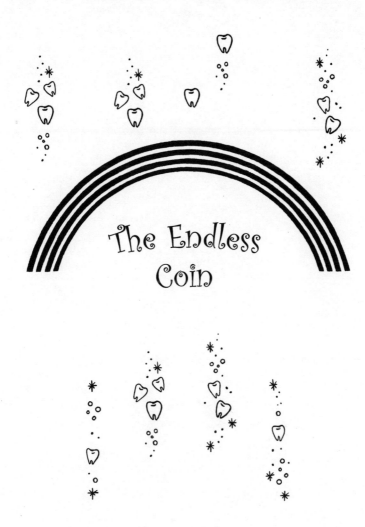

The Endless Coin

Contents

Things That Go Bump in the Night

Kirsty opened her eyes and blinked a few times. The bedroom was completely dark, and she could hear Rachel's steady breathing on the other side of the room. It was the middle of the night. What had woken her up?

Then she heard a soft scrabbling noise, and she felt her head lift up slightly.

Someone was pushing a hand under her pillow!

"Hey!" she exclaimed, sitting bolt upright in bed.

There was a muffled squawk from beside her bed, and something bumped into the bedside table.

"What's the matter?" asked Rachel,
instantly awake.

Kirsty had
recognised
the squawk.

"Rachel,
I think
there's a
goblin in
the room,
trying to steal
my tooth!" she said.

Rachel gasped and switched on her
bedside lamp. The girls looked around the
room, but everything looked exactly as
normal. There wasn't a goblin in sight.

"Are you sure you weren't dreaming?"
asked Rachel.

"I don't think so," said Kirsty.

She leaned down over the side of
the bed and peered into the darkness
underneath. The light from the bedside
lamp was dim, and at first she couldn't
see anything. Then she spotted two
greenish eyes glaring
at her out of
the shadows.

"He's
under
here!"
she cried.

Rachel
jumped out
of bed as the
goblin scurried
out from his

hiding place. He dived between her legs,
but his feet got tangled in the lamp cord.

There was another squawk and a crash, and the light went out. The girls heard him give a low groan. He had knocked the lamp onto his bony head.

"Don't let him get away!" said Kirsty, getting out of bed and feeling around the floor in the dark, trying to grab the goblin's feet.

"I don't know where he's gone!"
Rachel replied, stretching out her hands
at goblin height.

"Well, I've found the lamp," said Kirsty,
pressing the switch.
"And it works!"

The room was
flooded with
light again,
and the
girls looked
around.
The
goblin was
nowhere to
be seen.

"Let's check
under the beds,"
Rachel suggested.

They looked carefully, but he wasn't hiding under the beds. Rachel pulled the curtain aside and saw that the window was open.

"Perhaps he climbed out of the window and down the tree," she said. "Did he get your tooth?"

Kirsty felt under her pillow and smiled.

"No," she said, "it's still here."

At that moment, the bedroom door opened and Mr Walker's head appeared around it. He was blinking sleepily.

"Are you girls all right?" he asked. "We heard a crash."

"Sorry, Dad," said Rachel, climbing back into bed. "The bedside lamp got knocked over, but it's not broken."

"Well, turn out the light and go to sleep," Mr Walker replied. "It's the middle of the night, you know."

He went back to bed and Rachel switched off the lamp. No one had noticed that the wardrobe door was now slightly ajar. Kirsty and Rachel lay down and closed their eyes.

Buttons Barks a Warning!

The girls woke up late after their
midnight adventure. They dressed quickly
and hurried downstairs for breakfast. Mr
and Mrs Walker had already eaten, and
Mr Walker was putting on his shoes to go
to work.

"Morning, Dad," said Rachel, giving
him a kiss on the cheek. "Sorry we woke
you up last night."

"You must have been having a very exciting dream to knock your lamp over in your sleep!" he said with a laugh.

Rachel just smiled. She couldn't admit that it was really a goblin who had caused all the trouble. She had to let her dad believe that she had knocked over the lamp.

Just then, Buttons started to bark upstairs.

"Quiet, Buttons!" called Mr Walker. "Right, I'm off to work. Bye, girls!"

Rachel and Kirsty said goodbye and
then went into the kitchen. Rachel
poured out some cereal, and Mrs Walker
went out into the garden to hang out
some washing. Then, as Kirsty reached
for the cornflakes, the little white milk
jug on the breakfast table started to glow.
The girls knew at once that something
magical was about to
happen.

A puff of silver
fairy dust sparkled
from the top of
the jug, and
then Tamara
the Tooth
Fairy flew
out and gave
a little twirl.

She landed softly on the table in front of Rachel, and a little fairy dust sprinkled onto the tablecloth.

"Good morning!" she said in a bright voice. "I've come to tell you some news from Fairyland."

"Have you found your other magical objects?" asked Kirsty.

"Not yet," said Tamara. "But Fern the Green Fairy was visiting a tree near the Ice Castle, and she overheard some goblins talking. It's given me a clue at last! Jack Frost has sent one goblin to the human world with the endless coin.

He has ordered him to bring back as many teeth as he can find."

Rachel gave a little gasp.

"Tamara, there was a goblin in our room last night," she said.

They explained to Tamara what had happened in the middle of the night, and the little fairy's eyes shone with hope.

"If he was trying to take your tooth, he must have had the endless coin," she said. "It's magically impossible to take teeth from under pillows without it."

"But why does Jack Frost want so many teeth?" asked Kirsty.

"He wants to grind them down to make magic tooth dust," Tamara explained. "He thinks it will cure his toothache and protect him from getting it in the future."

Rachel opened her mouth to ask another question, but just then Buttons started to bark again. The girls looked at each other.

"That's Buttons's warning bark," said Rachel.

"There must be something wrong,"
Kirsty exclaimed, jumping to her feet.
"Come on!"

They raced up the stairs two at a time,
and Tamara zoomed above their heads.
Buttons was letting out a volley of loud,
deep barks that echoed around
the whole house.

"He's in your bedroom, Rachel!" said
Kirsty, racing into the room.

Buttons was standing in front of the wardrobe, barking with all his might. His tail was stiff and pointed, and the hair on his neck was standing up.

"What's the matter, Buttons?" Rachel asked, putting her hand on his soft head.

Buttons looked up at her and gave a little woof. Then he stared back at the wardrobe. The girls could now see that the door was very slightly ajar. They exchanged worried glances.

Then Rachel bravely stepped forward
and pulled the door wide open.

"EEEYOWEEE!"

A squealing, wailing bundle fell out of
the wardrobe, rolled across the floor and
landed at Rachel's feet!

The Bad-Tempered Bundle

The bundle jumped up, and the girls saw
that it had two spindly green legs, two
scrawny green arms and a very knobbly,
bony green head.

"It's a goblin!" cried Kirsty.

But he wasn't dressed in normal goblin style. He was wearing at least three skirts, two dresses, four pairs of trousers and a woolly hat, as well as two jumpers and a cardigan.

Rachel let out a cry of surprise. "He's wearing all my clothes from inside the wardrobe!" she exclaimed. "Take those off at once! They don't belong to you."

The goblin scowled at her.

"Shan't," he said, sticking out his tongue at her. "I'm not going to let that monster bite me! Its fangs will never get through all these layers."

"Buttons isn't a monster – he's my pet dog!" said Rachel. "And he would never bite anyone."

"I don't believe you," retorted the goblin rudely. "Go away and leave me alone, and take that monster with you."

"You can't order Rachel around in her own bedroom," said Tamara in an indignant voice. "You're the one who doesn't belong here, goblin."

"What are you going to do about it, you silly fairy?" the goblin demanded with a sneer. "You can't do anything because I've got your magic coin. HA!"

He blew a raspberry at her, and then touched his thumb to the tip of his crooked nose and waggled his fingers.

"Take off those clothes
at once and give the
endless coin back
to Tamara," said
Kirsty, putting
her hands on
her hips. "It's
wrong to take
things that don't
belong to you."

"You can't tell
me what to do," said
the goblin, sticking out
his bottom lip. "You're not
my boss. I'm on a special mission for Jack
Frost!"

Buttons took a step towards the goblin
and gave a low growl. He didn't like
anyone shouting at Rachel or Kirsty.

At once, the goblin jumped back into the wardrobe and let out a shriek of terror.

"Get it away from me!" he wailed. "I've been trapped in this stupid cupboard for hours. My neck hurts and my back hurts and I haven't even found one tooth for Jack Frost yet!"

"Give me back the endless coin and
I will use my magic to give you some
teeth," said Tamara.

The goblin peered out of the wardrobe
suspiciously.

"Really?" he asked.

"I promise," said Tamara.

The goblin grabbed
one of Rachel's
handbags from
inside the
wardrobe and
opened it. Then
he held up the
glimmering
endless
coin and
dropped it into
the handbag.

"Come and get it then," he said.

As Tamara darted towards the handbag, the girls saw the goblin smirk. There was a cunning flicker in his eyes. What was he planning?

"No!" cried Rachel.

"It's a trap!" Kirsty shouted at the same moment. "Stop!"

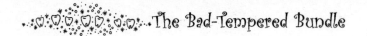

But they were both too late. Tamara flew into the handbag, and the goblin snapped it shut with a cackle of triumph. The Tooth Fairy was a prisoner!

Goblin on Wheels

"Why did you do that?" Rachel cried. "Tamara was offering to help you!"

"I don't want her help," the goblin said with a sneer. "Yesterday she sent three goblins back to Jack Frost with some chattering teeth that weren't even real. I'm not making the same mistake as they did! I'm too clever for you humans and fairies. You can't trick me!"

"Let her go right now," said Kirsty.

"No chance," said the goblin. "I'm taking her to the Ice Castle with me, and Jack Frost will keep her prisoner until she agrees to give him every tooth she can find."

Buttons growled again, and the goblin trembled. That gave Rachel an idea. She put her hand on Buttons's collar.

"I'll take Buttons into the next room if you'll let Tamara go," she said.

The goblin nodded eagerly. Rachel
opened the bedroom
door and took
Buttons into her
parents' room.
But as soon
as the dog
was out
of sight,
the goblin
gave a
squawking
laugh and
ran past Kirsty,
pushing her out
of the way. She fell
back onto Rachel's bed.

"Hey, stop!" cried Kirsty furiously. "We
had a deal!"

The goblin didn't reply. He ran down the stairs at top speed, clutching the handbag to his chest. Kirsty pulled herself up and ran out onto the landing, just in time to hear the front door slam shut.

"Rachel, come quickly!" she called. "He's getting away!"

Rachel dashed out of her parents' room. "We have to follow him!" she said. "We can't let him take Tamara to the Ice Castle. Come on!"

The girls raced downstairs, pulled on
their shoes and hurried outside. They
peered up and down the street.

"He's already disappeared!" said Kirsty
in alarm. "We're too late!"

"No, there he is!" Rachel cried,
pointing to the far end of the street. "I
just saw him duck down
behind that postbox."

They sprinted
up the street,
and the goblin
realised that
he had been
spotted. He
started to run
too, but his thick
layers of clothes
slowed him down.

Rachel's bobble hat was pulled down over his ears, her best long skirt billowed out behind him, and the handbag was clutched to his chest. He looked like a plump little old lady, and people turned around in surprise as he waddled past them as fast as he could go. The sun was already shining brightly, and the goblin was looking very hot and bothered.

"We're faster than him," said Kirsty, panting. "We've almost caught him!"

The goblin looked over his shoulder and gave a squawk of alarm. He ran up to a little boy who was playing with his scooter in the driveway of a house.

"Give me that!" he shouted, wrenching the scooter out of the boy's hands.

"That's mine!" wailed the little boy.

"Mine now!" sneered the goblin.

He jumped onto
the scooter and
disappeared
around the
corner at
top speed.
Kirsty and
Rachel
stopped
beside the
crying boy
and caught
their breath.

"That old lady took my scooter!" the little boy sobbed.

"Don't cry," said Rachel, feeling very sorry for him. "We'll try to get it back for you."

"But how are we going to do that?"

asked Kirsty. "We're not fast enough to catch up with him."

Rachel and Kirsty looked at each other in dismay. Whatever were they going to do now?

Four-Legged Hero

WOOF! WOOF!

There was a loud bark from behind the girls, and then Buttons raced past them. His ears streamed out behind him as he chased the goblin. He was running as fast as he could, and in seconds he had disappeared around the corner.

"Brilliant, Buttons!" shouted Rachel. "Come on, Kirsty!"

Buttons knew that the girls wanted to catch the goblin, and he was determined to do his best to help them. They sprinted after him and whizzed around the corner. They were just in time to see Buttons take a flying leap at the scooter!

The goblin was knocked onto the pavement. He was so wrapped up in Rachel's clothes that he bounced three times before rolling into the gutter.

He lay there
on his back,
waving
his arms
and legs
helplessly.
He
couldn't
get back
onto his feet!
Buttons stood
beside him, panting with his mouth
hanging open.

"He looks just as if he's laughing!"
said Kirsty, stopping to catch her breath.
"Good boy, Buttons!"

The handbag was lying on the
pavement beside the scooter. Rachel
ran to open it and Tamara zoomed out.

She had her wand in one hand, and the endless coin in the other. The coin had returned to fairy size, and Tamara was beaming from ear to ear.

"I knew you would rescue me!" she exclaimed.

"It wasn't us," said Rachel with a smile. "Buttons stopped the goblin and knocked him off the scooter."

Tamara gave Buttons a fairy kiss on the tip of his nose.

"Thank you, Buttons," she said. "You're a hero!"

Then she turned to the goblin and
waved her wand at him, saying a quick
spell.

"*Stealing Rachel's clothes was wrong,*
So send them back where they belong.
And give this dog a juicy bone
To have for tea when he gets home."

Instantly, the layers of clothes
disappeared, leaving the
goblin dressed in his own
short, ragged skirt.
He gave a loud
squawk and jumped
to his feet, shaking his
green fists at
them all.

"Give me that
tooth!" he shouted. "I
stole it fair and square!"

"This tooth belongs to Kirsty," said Tamara in a firm voice.

She placed the tooth in Kirsty's hand, and the goblin gave a yell. Then Buttons growled, and the goblin's knees knocked together.

"I'm not waiting around for that beast to bite me!" he declared.

He ran off and the girls sighed with relief.

"Thank goodness he's gone!" said Rachel.

"Can you take my tooth now that you've got the endless coin?" asked Kirsty hopefully.

Tamara's big smile faded slightly.

"I'm sorry," she said, "but I can't do anything with your tooth until I get the enchanted pouch back."

"We'll help you to find it," said Rachel. "Where shall we start?"

But at that moment, the girls heard Mrs Walker calling their names. Kirsty clapped her hand to her mouth.

"We just ran out without telling your mum where we were going!" she said to Rachel. "She must be worried about us."

"You should go home straight away, and I should take the endless coin back to Fairyland," said Tamara. "But I'll be back as soon as I can, and we can start our search for the enchanted pouch."

She waved her wand and disappeared in a flurry of golden sparkles. Kirsty picked up the fallen scooter, and Rachel patted Buttons. "Come on, boy, let's go home," she said.

"Tamara promised that there would be a nice bone waiting for you!"

The girls and Buttons hurried back to
Rachel's house. They stopped on the way
to return the scooter to the little boy,
whose tears dried at once.

Mrs Walker was standing in the front
garden, clipping a tree.

"Oh, did Buttons
run off?" she
asked. "I
thought it was
strange that
you didn't say
where you
were going!"

Rachel and
Kirsty just
smiled. They
couldn't tell her
the whole story!

They went through to the kitchen to finish their breakfast, and Buttons found a large, juicy bone in his bowl.

"What a great start to the day!" said Kirsty, pouring milk on her cornflakes.

"Yes, we've helped Tamara to find her second magical object, and it's not even nine o'clock yet!" said Rachel with a laugh. "I have a feeling that this is going to be a very good day!"

The Enchanted Pouch

Contents

Tamara's Request

"Good shot!" Rachel exclaimed. "You win!"

She picked up the shuttlecock and grinned at Kirsty. All afternoon, they had been playing badminton over an old tennis net in the back garden.

"Another game?" asked Kirsty. "We've each won five now. This can be the deciding match."

Mrs Walker leaned out of the kitchen window.

"Would you girls like a drink?" she called.

"In a minute, Mum," Rachel replied. "We're going to have another game first."

It was Kirsty's turn to serve. She held out the shuttlecock, aimed and then hit it with her racquet. The shuttlecock flew higher... and higher... and higher!

"Wow!" said
Rachel,
looking up
and shading
her eyes
from the sun.
"That was
an amazing
shot!"

"I can't even
see it," said
Kirsty, peering
into the clear
blue sky. "I've never
hit a shot like that before."

"There it is," said Rachel. "It's coming
back down."

"No…" said Kirsty. "I don't think that's
the shuttlecock. It's a different shape."

"You're right!" said Rachel in excitement. "It's Tamara!"

Tamara the Tooth Fairy swooped down and perched on the top of the net, fluttering her wings slightly to keep her balance.

"Hi, girls!" she said with a bright smile. "I've come to ask you a big favour."

Rachel and Kirsty dropped their racquets on the grass and ran up to the net.

124

"It's great to see you, Tamara," said Kirsty. "Have you found out where your enchanted pouch is?"

"Not exactly," said Tamara. "But I've been thinking about what the goblin said this morning. He told us that Jack Frost ordered him to collect teeth and bring them back to the Ice Castle. I'm sure that Jack Frost must have the enchanted pouch there with him."

"That makes sense," said Rachel. "The enchanted pouch is where your magic tooth dust is kept, and he must want to keep it as safe as possible."

"Yes," Kirsty agreed. "He thinks it will stop his toothache. How can we help?"

"Will you come to the Ice Castle with me?" asked the little fairy. "I have to find my enchanted pouch, but Jack Frost's home is a scary place.

126

I know you have both been there before, so I thought you might know the best places to look."

"Of course we'll come," said Rachel at once.

She looked up at the kitchen window, where her mum was washing up. Rachel knew that they wouldn't be missed, because fairy magic would make time stand still in the human world while they were away.

"Let's go down to the bottom of the garden," said Kirsty. "No one will be able to see us there."

As soon as they were out of sight of the kitchen window, Tamara raised her wand and a stream of glittering fairy dust whooshed from it, curling around the girls like a golden ribbon.

They felt a warm tingle as the fairy magic started to work. The garden around them disappeared, and gauzy wings appeared on their backs.

A few moments later the sparkles faded, and they found themselves flying over a forest of snow-covered trees. Ahead of them, a spiky castle was glittering with ice.

"Look, there's Jack Frost's home," said Rachel. "We're in *his* land now!"

A Toothache and a Teddy

Rachel, Kirsty and Tamara fluttered downwards to the edge of the forest. Their feet crunched the fresh snow as they landed.

"It's so cold!" said Tamara, rubbing her bare arms.

Rachel and Kirsty were already shivering. Tamara gave her wand a little flick, and instantly they were each snuggling into a thick faux-fur jacket.

"That's better," said Kirsty. "Now, how are we going to get into the Ice Castle?"

Hidden by the line of trees, they peered up at the turrets and battlements of Jack Frost's chilling home. Goblin guards were pacing up and down, keeping watch.

"I've never seen so many guards on the battlements," said Rachel. "Jack Frost must have something very precious inside — something that he wants to protect."

"Yes, my enchanted pouch," said Tamara, tightening her lips.

Kirsty was gazing at the smooth turrets when she saw a window being flung open, close to the top.

"Up there!" she exclaimed. "Someone has opened a window. Come on – that's our way in."

"What if one of the guards sees us?" asked Tamara.

"The goblins are usually too busy quarrelling with each other to look over the walls," said Rachel. "Besides, I think it's a chance we have to take."

Tamara nodded, and the three friends rose up into the air and flew as fast as they could towards the high turret. Blue curtains decorated with silver ice bolts were billowing out of the open window. Rachel, Kirsty and Tamara landed on the window ledge and slipped inside.

They could hear voices and a high-pitched whining sound.

"I wonder where we are," said Rachel.

She peered around the side of the curtain and drew in her breath sharply.

Then she turned to Kirsty and Tamara
and beckoned them over.

"We're in Jack Frost's bedroom!" she
whispered.

Kirsty and Tamara opened their eyes
wide and peeked around the side of the
curtain. Jack Frost was sitting up in bed.
A white cloth was wrapped under his
chin and tied
on top of
his head
in a large
bow.
He was
clutching
a spiky
teddy
bear and
whimpering loudly.

"That's the teddy that Sabrina the Sweet Dreams Fairy gave him," said Kirsty.

"What's wrong with him?" Rachel asked.

"He needs to have that tooth pulled out," said Tamara. "Poor Jack Frost – he looks as if he's in a lot of pain."

"I bet that hasn't made his temper any better," said Kirsty. "Look how the goblins are keeping their distance from him!"

At the farthest
end of the room
from the bed,
three goblins
were arguing
in loud voices.
They were all
wearing white
coats that were
much too big
for them.

"Those are
dentists' coats," said
Rachel. "I bet they stole them from the
dental surgery."

"He needs a special potion," said the
first goblin. "I think we should make a
magic brew of weeds and mud and onion
peel and mouldy berries."

"That won't help toothache," scoffed the second goblin. "That's for hiccups! He needs hot-water bottles strapped to his ears."

"Rubbish!" squawked the third goblin. "That tooth has gone bad. It needs to be pulled out."

"Yes!" said the first goblin. "Shall we knock it out with a hammer?"

"Don't be stupid," said the second goblin. "We need to use his wand and magic it out with a thunderbolt!"

"You're both wrong," the third goblin told them, putting his hands on his hips. "We just have to tie a piece of string around his tooth. Then we yank it out by tying the other end to the door handle."

"Ooh, that sounds like fun!" said the second goblin. "Let's try it!"

Uncle Jack Frost!

"I can't let them do this!" cried Tamara.

Before Rachel or Kirsty could stop her, she darted out from behind the curtain and fluttered into the centre of the room, facing the goblins.

"Stop!" she demanded. "I am the Tooth Fairy, and I can't let you do this terrible thing. Pulling teeth out with a piece of string is very wrong! You could make the pain even worse."

Jack Frost loosened the cloth around his head.

"I'm in agony!" he bellowed, then clutched his jaw and groaned. "It can't GET any worse!"

"A fairy!" squawked the goblins. "A fairy in Jack Frost's bedroom! Get her out!"

"You need to go
to the dentist,"
said Tamara,
turning to Jack
Frost. "That's
the only way
you'll get rid of
the pain."

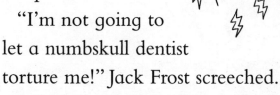

"I'm not going to
let a numbskull dentist
torture me!" Jack Frost screeched.

Rachel and Kirsty flew out to join their
friend.

"You should listen to Tamara," Kirsty
said. "She knows a lot more about teeth
than these goblins."

"No she doesn't!" shouted the first
goblin. "She hasn't even got a white
coat!"

"Listen to me," said Tamara, flying over to Jack Frost and landing on the blanket in front of him. "A dentist won't hurt you. They will make you feel better!"

Jack Frost stared at her. His face was screwed up in pain.

"I'm scared," he said in a small voice.

Rachel and Kirsty felt very sorry for him. They landed on the bed beside Tamara.

"Listen," said Rachel. "I've been going to the Tippington Dental Surgery all my life, and the dentist has never hurt me."

Jack Frost looked at her with a suspicious expression.

"Really?" he asked.

"I love going there," Rachel went on. "They use a special dye that makes your teeth go blue in the places where you haven't brushed properly."

"Yes, and the tooth polisher tickles and always makes me laugh," Kirsty added.

"And they give you a 'good patient' sticker at the end," said Rachel.

"We could take you to the Tippington Dental Surgery right now," said Tamara. "You could be out of pain within half an hour."

Jack Frost's eyes shone, and then he winced in pain again.

"All right!" he said. "I'll go. But if they hurt me, I'll blame you!"

"Fine," said Tamara. "First, you need to look like an ordinary human man."

She stroked her wand over Jack Frost's head, like a hairbrush. His spikes were smoothed down until they looked like hair, and his pyjamas were replaced by a T-shirt and jeans.

Then Tamara waved her wand. There
was a flash of bright silver light, and
Rachel and Kirsty closed their eyes.
When they opened them again, they
were hovering beside Tamara in an
alleyway, close to the Tippington Dental
Surgery. Jack Frost was
standing in front of
them, still clutching
his teddy.

"Are you
ready to go in?"
Tamara asked
him.

Jack Frost
shook his head.

"I can't," he
wailed. "It's too
scary!"

"Tamara, I've got an idea," said Kirsty. "If you turn us back into humans, we can pretend to be Jack Frost's nieces. Then we can go in with him and help him to be brave."

At once, Tamara waved her wand and returned the girls to human size. Kirsty and Rachel each took one of Jack Frost's arms. They marched him out of the alleyway, up the steps of the surgery and into reception.

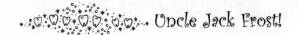

"Hello," said Rachel to the receptionist. "We need an emergency appointment, please. Our uncle has terrible toothache!"

A Brave
Patient

Jack Frost was very nervous, and he paced up and down in the waiting area, squeezing his teddy very hard. Luckily, they didn't have to wait for long. The door to the surgery opened, and the dentist looked out.

"Mr Frost?" she asked.

Jack Frost didn't move, but Rachel and Kirsty took his arms and led him gently into the surgery. The dentist raised her eyebrows. She raised them even higher when she saw the spiky teddy bear, but she didn't say anything about it.

"Let's see if I can take away your pain, Mr Frost," she said with a warm smile.

She guided him into the chair. There was a sailboat mobile dangling from the ceiling, with boats of red and blue swirling slowly around.

"Just lean back, look at the mobile and try to relax," said the dentist. "Open wide."

"Is it all right if we stay?" asked Kirsty. "Our uncle is a bit nervous."

"Of course," the dentist replied, peering into Jack Frost's mouth. "Goodness me, what spiky teeth you have, Mr Frost! But I see the problem tooth. I'll soon sort that out for you."

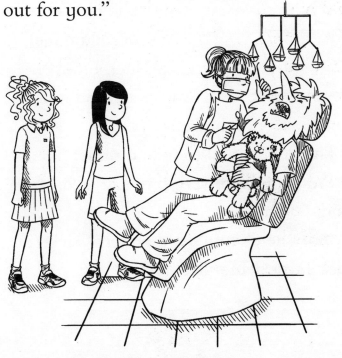

It was all over very quickly. The dentist pulled out the bad tooth, and gave Jack Frost some blue liquid to rinse out his mouth. Then she dropped the tooth into his hand.

"There you are," she said with a smile. "How do you feel now?"

"The pain's completely gone!" said Jack Frost. "I was very good and brave, wasn't I?"

The dentist had to hide a smile.

"Yes, you were very brave indeed," she said.

"So where's my 'good patient' sticker?" Jack Frost demanded.

"Well, they're usually just for our younger patients…" the dentist began.

"I AM young!" roared Jack Frost.

"He's back to his normal self already," whispered Rachel in Kirsty's ear.

The dentist gave Jack Frost a large 'good patient' sticker, and he stuck it proudly on his T-shirt.

"One for Teddy too," he snapped.

The dentist gave the teddy a sticker too. Then she handed Jack Frost a little bag.

"There is a toothbrush, some toothpaste and mouthwash in there," she said. "I would like you to brush your teeth twice a day from now on, and eat fewer sweets. I don't want to have to pull out any more of your teeth, Mr Frost!"

"Thank you very much," said Rachel, realising that Jack Frost wasn't going to be polite enough to say it.

The dentist opened the door and followed them out into the reception area.

"Has my next patient arrived?" she asked the receptionist.

"No," the receptionist replied. "That's the third person who hasn't turned up today. And you've had three more calls from patients you saw this morning, saying that their fillings have fallen out."

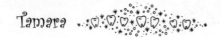

The dentist groaned, and Kirsty and Rachel looked at each other. They followed Jack Frost out of the surgery and down the steps.

"Things are going wrong for the dentist because you still have the enchanted

pouch," Kirsty said to him. "It's really unfair after she helped you so much."

Jack Frost was only half listening. He held up his tooth so that it gleamed in the sunshine, and gazed at it lovingly.

"Isn't it wonderful!" he said. "Nice and spiky! I'd much rather have this tooth than some pesky fairy's silly pouch."

"Do you mean that?" asked Rachel in an eager voice.

Was this their chance to get Tamara's enchanted pouch back?

The Magic of the Pouch

The girls pulled Jack Frost into the little alleyway where Tamara was waiting for them. He narrowed his eyes.

"If I give back the pouch, what do I get out of it?" he asked.

Rachel and Kirsty groaned. He was back to his old, mean self. But Tamara smiled at him.

"That's a wonderful tooth," she said. "It's one of the best I've ever seen."

Flattered, Jack Frost gave a smug little smile.

"If I had my enchanted pouch back, I could make you an icy display stand for the tooth," Tamara went on. "But I would need to use the special magic of the tooth dust in the pouch."

At once, Jack Frost reached into his pocket and pulled out a little velvet pouch. It glowed as he held it out to Tamara.

"Take it," he said. "I want a display stand!"

Tamara took the pouch, and a touch of her wand shrank it to fairy size. She pulled on the gold braid that held the pouch closed, and took a pinch of fairy dust from inside. Then she recited the words of a spell.

"Tooth dust old and tooth dust new
Use your power strong and true.
Give this tooth a place to sit
Where icy light can shine on it."

Tamara threw the fairy dust upwards, and it drew itself together, making a shape in mid-air. The shape grew more solid and then formed a splendid display stand, which landed on the ground in front of Jack Frost. It was a miniature version of his Ice Castle, complete with battlements and turrets. In the central turret was a tiny, blue, velvet cushion. Jack Frost gave a gasp of delight and placed his tooth on the cushion.

"I think he likes it," said Kirsty with a laugh.

Jack Frost pulled his wand from inside his T-shirt and tapped himself on the head. His hair sprang up into its usual spikes, and his blue cloak replaced his human clothes. Without even glancing at Rachel, Kirsty and Tamara, he flourished his wand. There was a loud thunderclap and a rush of icy wind, and then Jack Frost had disappeared with his tooth, his teddy and his display stand.

Tamara let out a big sigh of relief.

"He's gone back to his Ice Castle, thank goodness!" she said. "You were both brilliant! I couldn't have got my pouch back without you."

"We enjoyed it," said Kirsty with a giggle. "I'll never forget seeing Jack Frost get a 'good patient' sticker!"

"Thank you for everything," said Tamara. "It's time for me to go back to Fairyland, so goodbye - for now!"

She winked at them and then vanished in a little puff of fairy dust. Rachel and Kirsty smiled at each other. They knew what she meant!

That night, Kirsty went to sleep with her tooth under her pillow. When she woke up in the morning, she slipped her hand under her pillow and felt something that hadn't been there the night before. Kirsty drew her hand out slowly.

"What did Tamara leave for you?" asked Rachel, bounding over to her bed.

Kirsty opened her hand and the girls saw two objects lying there. One was a shiny pound coin. The other was a narrow silver ring, set with a tiny shimmering stone.

"Is it a pearl?" asked Kirsty, holding it up to the light.

The stone had transparent walls, and something inside was sparkling.

"No, it's not a pearl," said Rachel in excitement. "I know what it is! It's your own tooth, transformed into fairy dust!"

The girls shared a thrilled smile.

"This adventure has been a lot of fun," said Kirsty. "And now I'm really, really looking forward to losing my next tooth!"

Now it's time for Kirsty and Rachel to help...

Miranda
the Beauty Fairy

Read on for a sneak peek...

"This is amazing, Rachel!"

Her eyes wide, Kirsty Tate stared up at the enormous glittering steel and glass building in front of them. Across the entrance was a sign reading *Tippington Fountains Shopping Centre.*

"Yes, isn't it?" Rachel Walker agreed. "I'm so glad you're staying with me for half-term so that you could be here for the grand opening, Kirsty."

"Me, too," Kirsty said eagerly. "And I'm *really* looking forward to seeing Jessica

Jarvis!" The famous supermodel was the star guest at the new shopping centre's opening ceremony. Crowds of people had already gathered, waiting for the ceremony to begin.

"I think we're just in time for the parade," Mrs Walker said, locking her car. "Come along, girls."

Rachel, Kirsty and Mrs Walker hurried to join the crowd. Moments later the first float appeared around the side of the building.

"Every shop in the mall has its own float, Kirsty," Rachel explained. "Look, the first one is *Tippington Toys.*"

The float rumbled slowly towards them. A huge inflatable teddy bear sat on the back of the truck. Also on the float were two girls dressed as rag dolls with yellow wool pigtails and flouncy dresses, and a boy wearing a red soldier uniform. They waved to the crowds as they passed by.

"The next one is *The Book Nook*," Kirsty said, reading the painted banner strung across the float.

The Book Nook's float carried people dressed as characters from storybooks. The girls spotted Snow White, Cinderella and Pinocchio. This was followed by the *Sweet Scoop Ice Cream Parlour* float with its giant foam ice cream cones.

"Those ice creams look lovely!" Kirsty laughed.

Rachel sniffed the air. "I can *smell* something lovely, too," she said.

"So can I," Kirsty replied as delicious scents wafted past her nose. "Strawberries and vanilla!"

"The *Bath Bliss* float is coming," Mrs Walker said. "They sell hair and body products."

A banner flying across the float proclaimed *"We only use natural organic ingredients!"* Rachel and Kirsty laughed when they saw that the float was loaded with bubble machines spraying hundreds of shimmering, scented bubbles into the crowds.

"Magical!" Rachel sighed. She caught a strawberry-scented bubble on her finger before it popped gently. "They look like fairy bubbles, Kirsty!"

Read **Miranda the Beauty Fairy** to find out what adventures are in store for Kirsty and Rachel!

Meet the fairies, play games
and get sneak peeks at
the latest books!

www.rainbowmagicbooks.co.uk

There's fairy fun for everyone on
our wonderful website.
You'll find great activities, competitions, stories and
fairy profiles, and also a special newsletter.

Get 30% off all Rainbow Magic books at

www.rainbowmagicbooks.co.uk

Enter the code RAINBOW at the checkout.
Offer ends 31 December 2012.

Offer valid in United Kingdom and Republic of Ireland only.

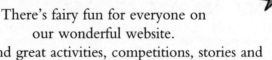

Competition!

Tamara the Tooth Fairy has created this special word wand just for you! Read the clues and put the correct answers in the teeth below. The last letter of each word is the start of the next one. When you have all three answers, go online and enter!

1. What is Tamara the Tooth Fairy holding on the front cover of the book?

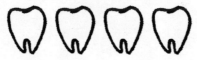

2. Which special doctor checks if your teeth are clean and healthy?

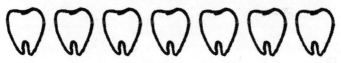

3. What do you use to clean your teeth?

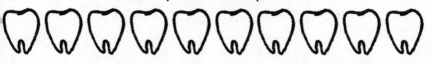

We will put all of the correct entries into a draw and select one winner to receive a special Rainbow Magic Goodie Bag featuring lots of treats for you and your fairy friends. You'll also star in a new Rainbow Magic story!

Enter online now at www.rainbowmagicbooks.co.uk

No purchase required. Only one entry per child. Two prize draws will take place on 30 September 2012 and 31 January 2013. Alternatively readers can send the three answers on a postcard to: Rainbow Magic Tamara the Tooth Fairy Fairy Competition, Orchard Books, 338 Euston Road, London, NW1 3BH. Australian readers can write to: RainbowMagic Olympia the Games Fairy Competition, Hachette Children's Books, Level 17/207 Kent St, Sydney, NSW 2000. Email: childrens.books@hachette.com.au. New Zealand readers should write to Rainbow Magic Olympia the Games Fairy Competition, 4 Whetu Place, Mairangi Bay, Auckland, NZ.

Meet the
Fashion Fairies

Miranda the Beauty Fairy

Claudia the Accessories Fairy

Tyra the Dress Designer Fairy

Alexa the Fashion Reporter Fairy

Matilda the Hair Stylist Fairy

Brooke the Photographer Fairy

Lola the Fashion Show Fairy

**If Kirsty and Rachel don't find the Fashion Fairies'
magical objects, Jack Frost will ruin fashion forever!**

www.rainbowmagicbooks.co.uk